To renew, find us online at:
https://capitadiscovery.co.uk/bromley

Please note: Items from the adult library
may also accrue overdue charges when
borrowed on children's tickets. 8/20

Enid Blyton®

THE SECRET SEVEN

HURRY, SECRET SEVEN, HURRY!

Illustrated by Tony Ross

Hodder
Children's
Books

THE SECRET SEVEN

PETER   JANET   JACK   COLIN

GEORGE   PAM   BARBARA

Have you read them all?

ADVENTURE ON THE WAY HOME

THE HUMBUG ADVENTURE

AN AFTERNOON WITH THE SECRET SEVEN

WHERE ARE THE SECRET SEVEN?

HURRY, SECRET SEVEN, HURRY!

THE SECRET OF OLD MILL

… now try the full-length **SECRET SEVEN** mysteries:

THE SECRET SEVEN

SECRET SEVEN ADVENTURE

WELL DONE, SECRET SEVEN

SECRET SEVEN ON THE TRAIL

GO AHEAD, SECRET SEVEN

GOOD WORK, SECRET SEVEN

SECRET SEVEN WIN THROUGH

THREE CHEERS, SECRET SEVEN

SECRET SEVEN MYSTERY

PUZZLE FOR THE SECRET SEVEN

SECRET SEVEN FIREWORKS

GOOD OLD SECRET SEVEN

SHOCK FOR THE SECRET SEVEN

LOOK OUT, SECRET SEVEN

FUN FOR THE SECRET SEVEN

SCAMPER

Hodder Children's Books
An imprint of Hachette Children's Group
Part of Hodder & Stoughton
Carmelite House
50 Victoria Embankment
London EC4Y 0DZ
An Hachette UK company

www.hachette.co.uk

CHAPTER ONE   9

CHAPTER TWO   17

CHAPTER THREE   27

CHAPTER FOUR   35

CHAPTER FIVE   45

CHAPTER SIX   51

CHAPTER SEVEN   61

CHAPTER EIGHT   67

CHAPTER ONE

The Secret Seven had been
out together for a picnic.
Scamper was with them,
his tail wagging happily. He
loved being alone with Peter

and Janet – but it was even better to be with the whole of the Seven! There was always somebody fussing over him, patting him, or talking to him.

'Well, I must say the baskets weigh a lot less coming home from a picnic than going to one!' said Janet, swinging hers to and fro. 'Oooh, sorry, Colin – didn't know you were just behind me.'

'You'd better give that basket to Scamper to carry,' said Colin. 'That's three times you've banged me with it.'

'Shall we go home through the fields or through the town?' said Peter.

'Through the town!' said everyone.

They were all thinking the same thing – what about a call at the ice cream shop?

So they went back through the town.

It was market day and the streets were full. People rushed about here and there, carrying parcels, calling to one another, and cars had to go very slowly indeed because there were so many people walking in the road.

A man came down the street, cycling quickly. He rang his bell as if he were in a great hurry, and people tried to get out of the way. Peter skipped to one side just in time as the man cycled past. He turned to stare after him indignantly.

'He almost knocked me over,' began Peter, and then stopped. Even as he spoke, something had happened.

CHAPTER TWO

Crash!

The man on the bicycle had bumped into a car and had been flung off into the road. A woman gave a loud scream and people hurried up at once.

The children ran to see what had happened. The man lay there, half dazed, his head badly bruised, and his cheek cut.

A policeman came up.

'He was going so *fast*,' said a woman nearby. 'He kept shouting to people to get out of the way. He was in an awful

hurry and didn't seem to see that car.'

The man tried to speak and the policeman bent down. He listened hard and looked puzzled. 'He keeps saying "Lever,"' he said. 'Is that his name? Does anyone know?'

More people crowded up and the policeman began to send them off. 'Now, now – move away,' he said. 'Ah, here's a doctor. *Will* you move away, you kids? Give the poor fellow a chance.'

The Secret Seven moved off with all the other children who had crowded round.

'I'll never ride *my* bicycle fast,' said Barbara. 'I never will, now I've seen how suddenly accidents can happen.'

'Who was the man? Do

you know?' asked Peter.

'I've never seen him before,' said Pam.

'Well, I seem to know his face,' said George, puzzled. 'Yes, I know I do. But I just can't think *who* he is.'

'*I* think I've seen him before, too,' said Jack, frowning. 'I've watched him doing something. What on earth can it be?'

'Oh, never mind,' said
Pam. 'What does it matter?
He's in safe hands now, with a
policeman there and a doctor.'

'I just *can't* remember,'
said George. 'It's no good. I
sort of feel he's something to
do with the railway. He's not
one of the porters, is he?'

'No,' said Jack, who
knew all the porters because
he so often went to meet his

father off the train. 'He's not a porter – he's not the ticket clerk either, or the station-master. All the same, I can't help thinking you're right – he is something to do with the railway.'

'Oh, stop bothering about it,' said Pam. 'I want to forget the accident. It was **horrid**.'

CHAPTER THREE

They walked along, swinging
their baskets and bags, Peter
and Colin arguing about
football, and the three girls
listening.

Suddenly George interrupted. '**I know**! I've remembered who that man is!' he said. 'And we're right – he is something to do with the railway.'

'Is his name Lever?' asked Janet.

'No,' said George. '"Lever" is part of his work, though. He's the man who pulls the lever in the signal box when

the train comes towards the railway station! You know – we've often watched him at the signal box, pulling the lever to swing the big gates open and then shutting them over the line when the train has passed.'

'Oh yes – of course! You're right,' said Jack. 'It's Mr Williams.'

'I say – I hope there's

someone at his cottage who will pull the lever to open the gates for the next train!' said Peter, stopping suddenly. 'That's why he was in such a hurry, I expect. He wanted to get back in time to open the gates.'

'The six-fifteen is due soon,' said Colin. 'My father's on it!'

'Let's go back quickly and

tell the policeman!' said Janet,
suddenly feeling worried at
the thought of a train racing
along the lines and crashing
into closed crossing gates.

'No time,' said Colin,
looking at his watch.

Peter made up his mind
quickly. 'This may be serious,'
he said. 'If there's no one at
the station house to pull the
lever for the next train, there'll

certainly be a smash. Even if the train doesn't rock off the lines, those big gates will be smashed to pieces. **Hurry up** – we'll run to the cottage and find out if anyone is there.'

CHAPTER FOUR

The seven children, with
Scamper racing behind
barking excitedly, ran down
the road and round the corner.
Down the next road and up

a little hill and down again –
and there, some way in front
of them, stretched the railway
line.

'Keep going!' panted
Peter. 'We're nearly there.
We've still got a few minutes
before the train is due.'

Peter reached the signal
box first. It stood opposite
the level crossing, a pretty
little place with a tiny garden

of its own.

Peter yelled as he ran up to it. 'Is there anyone at home! I say – is there anyone in?'

He banged at the door and then rang the bell beside it. Nobody answered.

Nobody came.

Then Colin ran to the window and looked inside. '**Anyone in**?' he shouted at the top of his voice. He turned

round. 'The signal box is empty!' he said. 'That's why Mr Williams was biking so fast to get back. He hadn't left anyone to see to the gates!'

'And that's why he kept saying "Lever! Lever!"' said Janet. 'What are we to do?'

'Pull the lever and open the gates ourselves, of course,' said Peter, trying to be as calm as possible. He could see that the others were getting excited and alarmed. That would never do. Everyone must keep calm, everyone must help. They needed to get into the signal box as quickly as possible.

Colin looked round to see if anyone was near who could help them. A strong adult would be most

welcome! But not a soul was there except a small girl, who stared at them solemnly all the time.

'George, Janet! Come with me to the nearest gate and help me to open it!' shouted Peter. 'Jack, you go to the other one with Pam and Barbara and Colin. And for goodness' sake, hurry up! The train's due in about a minute!'

'We must all look out for it!' shouted Colin. 'It will be down on us at top speed before we know where we are!'

CHAPTER FIVE

Soon all seven children were working hard to find a way into the signal box. Peter pushed at the door whilst the others searched the windowsills and the flower beds for a spare key. It couldn't only be Mr Williams who had a key!

'I can hear the train!' yelled Janet, who had very sharp ears. 'And the lines are beginning to tremble. Hurry, hurry!'

Colin was searching by the door when he found an upturned flowerpot. Inside, taped to the bottom, was a key.

'I've found it!' Colin called out with excitement.

'The **train's coming**!' shouted Pam. 'The **train's coming**! Get inside, Peter, **get inside**!'

Yes – the train was certainly coming. It whistled as it came roaring along, and when Peter looked up he could see it tearing down the line.

By this time, Colin had

got the signal box door open.
Peter raced inside and found
the lever. He grabbed it and
pulled with all his might. Yes,
the gates were opening! The
train would be fine!

Pam **shouted** again as
the engine raced past, making
quite a wind. Then the long
row of swaying carriages came
rumbling past, making a truly
enormous noise.

CHAPTER SIX

In a few moments the train
had drawn into the station.
People began to get off, all
looking forward to getting
home after a long day at work.

Colin's father would be folding up his evening paper, ready to get off.

'I feel rather faint,' said Barbara suddenly, and sat

down against next to the lever.
'Oh dear – how silly.'

'It's just the excitement,'
said Peter, whose heart was
thumping so hard in his chest
that he found it quite difficult
to speak. 'My word, we didn't
have much time. But we just
did it!'

A shout came to their
ears, and they turned. It was
the policeman on a bicycle,

with two or three men behind
in a car.

'Hey – what are you
doing on the lines, you
children? Did anything
happen to the gates?'

'No. We managed to open
them for the train,' shouted
back Peter.

'Well, I'm amazed,' said
the policeman, getting off
his bicycle as the three men

jumped out of their car.

'Did you remember the lever when you found out who that man was who was knocked down?' asked Peter.

'Yes – the fellow managed to tell us at last,' said the policeman. 'I shot off at once – and these men came in their car as soon as they could. My word – when I saw the train racing by, I thought everything was up! I listened for the gates to be smashed – but no, the train just raced by as usual.'

'You mean to say you kids thought of the lever?' said one of the other men. 'How did you think of such a thing?'

'We remembered who that man was – Mr Williams, the crossing gates man,' said George. 'Then we thought of the gates – and the train that was due – and we ran like hares to get to the signal box.'

'We only *just* managed it,' said Jack. 'Whew – I'm dripping wet! It was a long run!'

'I'm melting, too!' said Barbara, who was still sitting down, but already looking a little better.

CHAPTER SEVEN

'Who *are* you children?' said
another man, a big, burly
fellow, looking at them
hard. 'You seem a jolly good
bunch of kids, I must say!

You've probably saved a lot of damage, you know.'

'We're the Secret Seven,' said Peter proudly, and tapped his badge. 'Ready to do any job of work, at any time!'

'So I see,' said the man. 'Well, I'm a railway official, so you can take it from me that you've saved us pounds and pounds of damage by opening those gates – besides possibly a nasty accident. The train *might* have swerved off the rails when it hit the gates.'

'I'm jolly glad it didn't,' said Colin. 'My father's on that train! Wait till I tell him our tale tonight!'

'Well, before you do that, I'd like you to do something else for me, if you will,' said the big man, and winked at his two companions.

'What's that?' asked
Peter, with visions of another
exciting bit of work to do.

'Help me to eat a few ice
creams!' said the man. 'You
look so hot – you ought to
cool down. And that would be
a good way of doing it – don't
you think so?'

'**Oooh yes**!' said
everyone, and Barbara stood
up at once. She felt quite

prepared to eat at least three ice creams if this man offered them!

CHAPTER EIGHT

The two men with him went to swing the gates back across the lines again, so that people might pass over on foot or in cars. The big man got into his car, and told the children to follow him to the ice cream shop just down the road.

Soon they were all sitting together, with such enormous ice creams that they really couldn't believe their eyes.

'This is the biggest ice cream I've ever had in my life,' said Peter.

'You deserve it, old son,'

said the big man, who was eating an ice cream, too. 'How in the world did you open those gates in time? You had only a few minutes to race away from Williams, get into the signal box, and pull the lever. I don't know how you did it!'

'Yes – you're right,' said Peter, thinking about it. 'I don't quite know how we did it, either. But the thing is – we did it!'

Well, that's really all that matters, Secret Seven. You saw what had to be done – and **you did it**!

LOOK OUT FOR ANOTHER
SECRET SEVEN
COLOUR SHORT STORY ...

THE SECRET OF OLD MILL

Peter and Janet think Old Mill is
perfect for their Seven Society
meetings — until they make a
startling discovery about some stolen
goods. The gang hatch a plan to wait
for the thieves to come back ...

THE SECRET SEVEN ONLINE

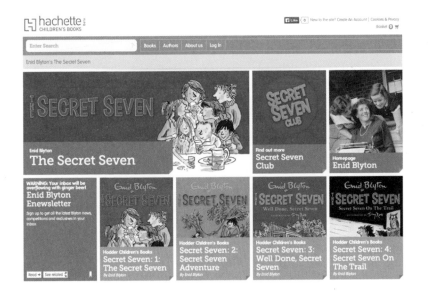

ON THE WEBSITE, YOU CAN:-

- Download and make your very own **SECRET SEVEN** door hanger
- Get tips on how to set up your own **SECRET SEVEN** club
- Find **SECRET SEVEN** snack recipes for your own club meetings
- Take the **SECRET SEVEN** quiz to see how much you really know!
- Sign up to get news of brilliant competitions and more great books

AND MUCH MORE!

GO TO ... **WWW.THESECRETSEVEN.CO.UK** AND JOIN IN!

START YOUR
SECRET SEVEN CLUB

In each of the Tony Ross editions of The Secret Seven is a Club Token (see below).
Collect any five tokens and you'll get a brilliant Secret Seven club pack –
perfect for you and your friends to start your very own secret club!

GET THE SECRET SEVEN CLUB PACK:

| 7 club pencils | 7 club bookmarks | 1 club poster | 7 club badges |

Simply fill in the form below, send it in with your
five tokens, and we'll send you the club pack!

Send to:

**Secret Seven Club, Hachette Children's Group,
Marketing Department, Carmelite House,
50 Victoria Embankment, London, EC4Y 0DZ**

Closing date: 31st December 2016

TERMS AND CONDITIONS:

(1) Open to UK and Republic of Ireland residents only (2) You must provide the email address of a parent or guardian for your entry to be valid (3) Photocopied tokens are not accepted (4) The form must be completed fully for your entry to be valid (5) Club packs are distributed on a first come, first served basis while stocks last (6) No part of the offer is exchangeable for cash or any other offer (7) Please allow 28 days for delivery (8) Your details will only be used for the purposes of fulfilling this offer and, if you choose [see tick box below], to send email newsletters about Enid Blyton and other great Hachette Children's books, and will never be shared with any third party.

- ✂ - - - - - - - - - - - - - - - - - -

Please complete using capital letters (UK Residents Only)

FIRST NAME:

SURNAME:

DATE OF BIRTH: DD MM YYYY

ADDRESS LINE 1:

ADDRESS LINE 2:

ADDRESS LINE 3:

POSTCODE:

PARENT OR GUARDIAN'S EMAIL ADDRESS:

☐ I'd like to receive a regular Enid Blyton email newsletter and information
about other great Hachette Children's Group (I can unsubscribe at any time).

I SECRET SEVEN CLUB TOKEN

www.thesecretseven.co.uk